"Breath? YUK! Oh, well. Maybe they won't notice."

The first day at a new school is always hard. But it is even harder when you're a zombie. Sam started getting ready hours ago.

"This is Sam," said Mr Broad.
"He's new. I want you to make
him feel welcome."

10

"Yeah, right!" said Clogger Mills,
the class bully.

12

Later on at break time things didn't get any better...

"Let's have some fun with the new jerk," said Clogger Mills.

He put his foot out. Sam tripped over it.

Oh, no! thought Sam. *I'm going to fall apart!*

But Sam's new friends were fast.

17

"Why don't you leave the new guy alone?" said Danny.

But Clogger just laughed.

Then Lin had an idea.

23

29